THREE LITTLE PIGS

Retold by Heather Amery
Illustrated by Stephen Cartwright

Language Consultant: Betty Root

There is a little yellow duck to find on every page.

Once upon a time, there was a Mother Pig who had three baby Pigs and they all lived together in a tiny little house.

The baby Pigs grew and grew until, one day, Mother Pig said, "You're too big for my tiny house. It is time you had houses of your own."

Next day Mother Pig packed up a bundle of food for each little Pig and off they trotted down the road.

"Goodbye, dear children," said Mother Pig, waving to them. "Build your houses well and, remember, never open the door to the Big, Bad Wolf. He would like to eat you."

Soon the first little Pig met a man carrying a huge bundle of straw.

"Please, sir," said the Pig, "will you give me some straw so I can build a little house of my own?"

"Yes," said the man, and gave him a big bundle.

The little Pig began to build his house of straw. He worked very hard, and by the end of the day, he had finished his lovely little house. It had a big door at the front, a little door at the back, and two small windows.

"Now I will be safe and snug inside," he said.

The second little Pig trotted down the road and met a man carrying a huge load of sticks.

"Please, sir," he said, "will you give me some sticks so I can build a little house of my own?"

"Why, of course," said the man and he gave the little Pig lots of strong sticks.

All day the little Pig worked and worked. When he had finished, he had a lovely little house with strong walls, a roof, two doors, two windows and a chimney.

"This will keep the Big, Bad Wolf out," he said, "and I will be safe and snug inside."

The third little Pig trotted down the road and met a man with a huge load of bricks.

"Please, sir," said the little Pig, "will you give me some bricks so I can build a little house of my own?"

"Certainly," said the man and gave him a lot.

For days the little Pig worked and worked. He built the walls, put on the roof and fitted in the windows. When he had finished, he had a lovely little house with thick walls, a big chimney, two doors and two windows.

"I'm not afraid of the Big, Bad Wolf," he said.

One day, the Wolf knocked on the door of the straw house. "Little Pig, let me in," he said, "or I'll huff and I'll puff and I'll blow your house down."

"No, Mr Wolf, I won't let you in," said the Pig. So the Wolf huffed and puffed and he blew the house down.

The little Pig ran all the way to the stick house.

But soon the Wolf came knocking on the door.

"Little Pig, let me in," he said, "or I'll huff and I'll puff and I'll blow your house down."

"No, no, Mr Wolf, we won't let you in," said the two little Pigs.

The Wolf huffed and puffed and blew the house down.

The two little Pigs ran as fast as they could all the way to the brick house. But soon the Wolf came knocking on the door.

"Little Pig, let me in," he said "or I'll huff and I'll puff and I'll blow your house down."

"No, no, we won't let you in," said the Pigs. So the Wolf huffed and puffed and puffed and huffed.

And he huffed and puffed and puffed and huffed but he could not blow the house down. He was very hungry and very out of breath. He prowled around the house, looking for a way in.

Then the Wolf jumped up on the roof and
looked down the chimney. The three little Pigs
quickly lit a big fire in the stove and put a huge pot,
full of water, on it.

"Now we're ready for the Big, Bad Wolf," they
said, and waited for him.

The Wolf slid down the chimney and fell into the pot of water with a big splash. One little Pig quickly put the lid on the pot and another tucked in the Wolf's tail.

"That's the end of the Big, Bad Wolf," they said and the three little Pigs danced with joy.

"Now we'll have supper," said the third little
Pig, "and you can both stay with me in my little
brick house."

After supper, the three little Pigs went to bed,
safe and snug, and happy that the Big, Bad Wolf
would never, ever frighten them again.

First published in 1988 by Usborne Publishing Ltd, 83-85 Saffron Hill, London EC1N 8RT, England.
Copyright © 1993, 1988 Usborne Publishing Ltd.